Goldilocks
and the Three Bears

PC
TREASURES, INC.

Published by

PC Multimedia Entertainment
TREASURES, INC.

2765 Metamora Road, Oxford, Michigan 48371 USA

Goldilocks and the Three Bears
Adapted by Larry Carney
Illustrated by Marco Arantes
Audio CD Reading Performed by Kara Kimmler
Songs Written by Larry Carney
Songs Produced and Performed by D. B. Harris

ISBN 1-60072-034-X

First Published 2007.

Made in China.

Once upon a time there was a cozy cottage in the woods. In this cottage lived three bears. There was a great big Papa Bear. There was a medium-sized Mama Bear. And there was a little Baby Bear.

TURN PAGE

The three bears were a very happy family. Every day they would eat porridge and relax in their comfortable chairs. They really enjoyed being together.

One morning the bears sat down
to eat a breakfast of porridge. But the
porridge was too hot to eat.

TURN PAGE

Papa Bear looked at his family and said, "Say, why don't we go for a walk? When we return, our porridge will have cooled off enough for us to eat." The three bears rose from the table and went for a pleasant stroll in the forest.

At the edge of the forest was a pretty
little house. In this house lived a little
girl named Goldilocks. Goldilocks was a
very nice child. She was always polite
and always listened to her parents.

One morning Goldilocks went outside to pick some flowers. She was not supposed to go into the forest, but when she saw some pretty flowers growing a little ways in the woods, she decided to go and pick them.

In the forest she saw more pretty
flowers to pick, so she walked a little
further into the woods. Then, deeper
in the forest, she saw even more pretty
flowers. So again she walked a little
further into the woods to pick them.

Soon Goldilocks' hands were full of flowers and she decided to go back home. But she had wandered so far into the forest that she had gotten lost.

Goldilocks started walking, hoping
that she would, in time, come to the
edge of the forest. So on she walked,
on and on, without stopping to rest.

After a while Goldilocks came to a little cottage. She knocked on the door and said, "Hello!" but there was no answer. Goldilocks was getting worried about being lost. So even though she knew it was wrong to go into someone else's house without being invited, she opened the door and went inside.

No one was inside the cottage so
Goldilocks looked around. She went
into the kitchen and saw three bowls
of porridge on the table. She knew it
was wrong to eat someone else's food,
but she was so hungry that she decided
to have a taste.

The porridge in the first bowl was too hot. The porridge in the second bowl was too cold. But the porridge in the third bowl was just right. Before she knew it, Goldilocks had eaten all the porridge in the bowl.

After eating, Goldilocks felt like relaxing. In the living room she found three chairs. She knew it was wrong to sit in someone else's chair without asking, but she was so worn out that she decided to sit down and relax for a little while.

The first chair was too hard. The second chair was too soft. But the third chair was just right. Goldilocks sat in the chair for a while, but she was too heavy for it and the chair broke in pieces.

Goldilocks was getting sleepy now. She walked into the bedroom and saw three beds. She knew it wasn't nice to take a nap in someone else's bed, but she was very tired. The first bed was too hard. The second bed was too soft. But the third bed was just right. Goldilocks soon fell fast asleep. About this time the three bears came home.

TURN PAGE

BABY

The three bears went into the kitchen to eat their porridge. Papa Bear looked at his bowl and said, "Somebody's been eating my porridge!" Mama Bear said, "Somebody's been eating my porridge!" Baby Bear frowned and said, "Somebody's been eating my porridge – and ate it all up!"

The three bears went into the living room. Papa Bear said, "Somebody's been sitting in my chair!" Mama Bear said, "Somebody's been sitting in my chair!" Baby Bear looked at his chair that was lying in pieces on the floor and cried, "Somebody's been sitting in my chair— and it's broken!"

TURN PAGE

The three bears decided to look around the cottage to see if anything else was out of place. They went into the bedroom. Papa Bear said, "Somebody's been sleeping in my bed!" Mama Bear said, "Somebody's been sleeping in my bed!"

Little Baby Bear looked at his little bed and said, "Somebody's been sleeping in my bed—and she's still sleeping in my bed!" The bears stood around the bed and looked at the sleeping Goldilocks.

"Why, it's a little human child!" Said Papa Bear. At the sound of his voice, Goldilocks woke up. She was very scared when she saw the bears standing over her. Mama Bear smiled at Goldilocks and said, "Don't worry little one, we won't harm you." "Y-you won't?" Goldilocks asked. Papa Bear chuckled and said, "Oh, goodness no."

Goldilocks told them how she had wandered into the woods to pick flowers and had gotten lost. Papa Bear told Goldilocks that she should never go wandering into the woods by herself and that she should always make sure her mother and father know where she is.

Goldilocks thought of her mother and father and tears began to run down her cheeks. "Oh, I'm going to be lost forever!" Papa Bear said, "Now, now, little one, don't cry. Why, we'll help you get back home." "Really?" asked Goldilocks. "Why, of course! No one knows these woods better than we bears! You'll be home before you know it!"

Goldilocks and Baby Bear climbed up on Papa Bear's back and they all walked into the woods. After walking for a long, long time, they stopped. Papa Bear pointed with his great big paw and said, "Is that your house over there Goldilocks?" Goldilocks smiled brightly and said joyfully, "Oh, Yes!"

"Thank you so much for helping me." Goldilocks said with a smile. The three bears smiled at their new little friend. "Goodbye Goldilocks!" They said with a wave of their paws as they headed happily back into the woods.

Collect Them ALL!

Goldilocks and the Three Bears

The Little Mermaid

Hansel and Gretel

The Three Little Pigs

Little Red Riding Hood

The Ugly Duckling

The Gingerbread Man

Billy Goats Gruff

Plus Many More

See them all and much more at
www.ToteBooks.com